Hattie and the Higgledy-Piggledy Hedge

Hattie and the Higgledy-Piggledy Hedge

Carol Bland Dolson

Illustrated by Elaine Hearn Rabon

JONQUIL BOOKS   ATHENS, GEORGIA

Published by Jonquil Books, an imprint of Miglior Press

Athens, Georgia

www.migliorpress.com

Printed in the United States of America

ISBN 978-0-9827614-4-1

10 9 8 7 6 5 4 3 2 1

First Edition

For Angela, Jennifer, and Anne

Hattie's mother was an artist. Hattie's grandmother was an artist. And Hattie wanted to be an artist, too.

Hattie's father was a gardener. Hattie's grandfather was a gardener. Hattie liked to garden, too. But she wanted to be an artist more than anything in the world. She wanted to be the best artist she could be.

Hattie's grandparents lived in a cottage in the countryside. When time came to visit them, Hattie packed her paint box first thing. "Every day, I will paint along with Grandmother," she said. "By the end of the week, I will surely be a better artist."

Grandmother painted in the sunny conservatory. It was full of paint pots and brushes, canvases and easels, and rags that smelled like turpentine.

Outside in Grandfather's garden, there were sweet-smelling blossoms. They were as bright as the colors on Grandmother's palette. There was also a higgledy-piggledy hedge that made you laugh just to look at it. It dipped a little here. It bulged a little there. It had humps and bumps just everywhere.

Before she went to bed, Hattie laid out old clothes. The kind you can spill paint on and it doesn't matter. She got her paint box ready, too. She wanted to get an early start in the morning.

On Monday morning, Hattie wanted to be the best artist she could be. But Grandfather said, "Shouldn't we be in the garden this sunny day?" So off they went.

"Something must be done about that higgledy-piggledy hedge," Grandfather said. "But I must clean and tidy the fish pool. In a proper garden, visitors enjoy seeing happy fish swimming in water clean and clear."

Hattie helped Grandfather for a while. Then she stared at the higgledy-
piggledy hedge. Suddenly she thought of something. She grabbed the small
shears that Grandfather gave her and went to work. She snipped a little
here. She clipped a little there. She cut and shaped just everywhere. When
she finished, she was pleased. But Grandfather didn't seem to notice.

On Tuesday morning, Hattie wanted to be the best artist she could be.
But before she could join Grandmother in the conservatory, she met
Grandfather. "Would you help me in the garden this sunny day?" he asked.
So off they went.

"Something must be done about that higgledy-piggledy hedge," Grandfather
said. "But I must prepare a bed for the annuals. In a proper garden, visitors
admire beds where flowers bloom all summer long."

Hattie helped Grandfather plant colorful flowers in the rich, dark earth. "Just like a patchwork quilt," she thought. Then she found the small shears and went to work on the hedge. She snipped a little, clipped a little, cut and shaped. When she finished, she was pleased. But Grandfather didn't notice. He was busy gathering up his tools.

On Wednesday morning, Hattie wanted to be the best artist she could be.
But before she could open her paint box, Grandfather waved. "Come along
to the garden. We must not waste this fine sunny day." So off they went.

"Something must be done about that higgledy-piggledy hedge," Grandfather
said, not glancing that way. "But this old stone urn needs a rose tree
growing up and lots of ivy trailing down. In a proper garden, visitors always
appreciate a handsome garden urn with ivy trailing down."

Hattie watched for a while as Grandfather carefully nestled the plants into the old stone urn. Then she took the small shears and went to work on the hedge. She snipped, clipped, cut, and shaped. When she finished, she was pleased. But Grandfather didn't look her way.

On Thursday morning, Hattie wanted to be the best artist she could be.
But before she could squeeze out one squiggle of paint from a shiny tube,
Grandfather peeped around the door. "A surprise is waiting in the garden on
this sunny day," he said. "Come see." So off they went.

"Something must be done about that higgledy-piggledy hedge," Grandfather
said. "But first, see this funny old gargoyle? It must be fastened to the rain
pipe. A funny gargoyle adds a bit of interest to a proper garden. It always
amuses people visiting there."

Hattie studied the gargoyle while Grandfather fetched the ladder. Then she took her small shears and went to work on the hedge. Snip . . . clip . . . cut . . . shape. When she finished, she was pleased. But Grandfather said nothing at all.

On Friday morning, Hattie wanted to be the best artist she could be. But as Grandmother helped her set up the smallest easel, Grandfather rushed in. "Hurry along to the garden," he said. There's much to do there this sunny day." So off they went.

"Something must be done about that higgledy-piggledy hedge," Grandfather said as he hurried along the opposite path. "But I must start planting the catmint and wallflowers and Michaelmas daisies. They will attract more butterflies. In a proper garden, visitors are delighted to see fluttering butterflies."

Hattie helped Grandfather dig holes for a while. Then she took her small shears and went to work on the hedge. She snipped a little here. She clipped a little there. She cut and shaped just everywhere. When she finished, she was pleased. But Grandfather didn't notice. He seemed interested only in the butterflies hovering over the new plants.

On Saturday morning, Hattie wanted to be the best artist she could be. But she did not go to the conservatory. She felt much too tired to paint a beautiful picture.

"I'll just watch Grandfather work in the garden this sunny day," she thought. But Grandfather wasn't working. He was busy serving morning coffee and rich, crumbly shortbread to a garden full of people.

The visitors seemed to enjoy the happy fish swimming in the water clean and clear. They admired the colorful annual bed where flowers bloom all summer. They appreciated the handsome garden urn with ivy trailing down. They were amused by the funny gargoyle. They were delighted with the fluttering butterflies. But when they came to the higgledy-piggledy hedge, they stopped. They stared. They smiled.

The old hedge still dipped a little here. It still bulged a little there. It still had humps and bumps just everywhere. But now it was different.

"A very special artist created this masterpiece," said Grandmother.

"All proper gardens should have a hedge such as this," said Grandfather.

All of the visitors to the garden agreed.

On Sunday morning, Hattie still wanted to be the best artist she could be. "I am determined to paint a beautiful picture this sunny day," she said. And she did. She painted a picture of the higgledy-piggledy hedge.

THE END